Bambi

THE WONDERFUL WINTER TREE

By Elizabeth Spurr

Illustrations by DRI Artworks

Bambi awoke one morning to find a white blanket covering his whole world.

"This is snow," explained his mother. "It means winter is upon us."

"Snow?" said Bambi. He walked around in a circle and felt the cold snow crunch under his hooves. "I like snow."

"Snow is pretty to look at, but winter can be hard," said his mother. "Especially when we animals can't find food."

Just then Thumper the rabbit called to Bambi from a frozen pond nearby. "Hiya, Bambi! Why dontcha come sliding? Look, the water's stiff!"

Bambi nuzzled his mother good-bye and pranced off to join his friend.

On Bambi's way to the pond, he bumped into his pal, Flower. "You wanna come skating?" Bambi asked. "The water's stiff."

"No, thanks," said the skunk. "I'm ready to settle down for a long winter nap."

Then Bambi spotted a squirrel, standing in the hollow of an oak tree. "The pond is stiff. Come sliding," Bambi called.

"Thanks, but I'm storing nuts for the long winter," said the busy squirrel.

The chipmunk was in his nest, and the bear was asleep in his cave. Bambi went to the pond alone, where he found Thumper whooping it up with his rabbit friends, sliding happily across the ice.

But, for Bambi, the skating was neither as much fun nor as easy as it looked. After dozens of flops on the slippery ice, he was both sore and hungry. So, Bambi set off to find his mother.

"I'm hungry," Bambi said when he saw his mother.

"Today we'll have to search for our dinner," Bambi's mother said.

Following his mother, Bambi poked through the powdery snow until he thought his nose would freeze. He finally uncovered a mound of green grass. Bambi's mother watched over him as he ate.

Then Bambi and his mother curled up in the thicket for a long nap, their bodies huddled against the chilly air. Before falling asleep, Bambi turned to his mother. "Will winter be over soon?" he asked.

"It seems long, but it won't last forever," his mother replied, hoping to comfort her young son.

Day after day, the animals spent most of their time in search of food. Bambi and his mother scoured the forest, sometimes with little luck.

"Mother," asked Bambi, "is this why the birds fly south, and why our other friends sleep through the winter?"

His mother nodded yes and gently nuzzled him.

One day, Bambi found little to eat except some bitter bark. Then, at the edge of the valley, he, his mother, and Thumper came upon a wondrous sight— a tall, snow-covered pine tree, draped top to bottom with strings of berries and popcorn. From each branch hung a ripe green apple.

"Wow!" cried Thumper.

Slowly, cautiously, the group moved closer.

"What is it, Mother?" asked Bambi.

"The most beautiful tree I've ever seen," she said. "He must have known that this was your first Christmas, Bambi."

"Who, Mother?" Bambi was so hungry, he could almost taste the juicy apples.

"Santa Claus," Thumper explained.

"Santa Claus?" said Bambi. "Who's that? And what's a Christmas?"

Thumper and Bambi's mother explained that Santa was a jolly, magical elf who visited just around the time of the first snowfall each year.

"He travels in a great big sleigh pulled by reindeer and delivers presents and holiday cheer," Thumper said.

"It was Santa who hung those berries and apples," continued Thumper.

"Wow, I like this Santa elf," Bambi said with a giggle.

After calling the good news to the other animals, Bambi, his mother, and Thumper began to share the feast.

As they ate, they noticed a bright star in the heavens. And while it shone, a peaceful hush settled over the valley.

As Bambi gazed at the star in the sky, his heart swelled with the hope that spring would soon arrive.